Magic Animal Friends

Special thanks to Valerie Wilding

ISBN 978-0-545-94078-8

Series author: Daisy Meadows

10 9 8 7 6 5 4 3 2 1 16 17 18 19 20

Printed in the U.S.A. 40
First printing 2016

Chloe Slipperslide's Secret

Daisy Meadows

Scholastic Inc.

Honey Tree
Sunshine Meadow
Mr. Cleverfeather's Inventing Shed
Goldie's Grotto
Toadstool Café
Toadstool Glade
Parasol Tree
Mrs. Taptree's Library
Library
Friendship Tree
Grizelda's Workshop
Sparkl
Falls
Rushing Rapids
Entrance to the Caverns
Butterfly Bowery
Nibblesqueak Bakery

Map of Friendship Forest

Can you keep a secret? I thought you could!

Then I'll tell you about an enchanted wood.

It lies through the door in the old oak tree.

Let's go there now—just follow me!

We'll find adventure that never ends,

And meet the Magic Animal Friends!

Love,

Goldie the Cat

Contents

CHAPTER ONE

Off to Friendship Forest!

"Look at that!" said Lily Hart, pointing to all the autumn leaves floating on Brightley Stream. "It can't be much fun for the fish and frogs with all those in the water."

Her best friend, Jess Forester, joined her

on the bank of the stream. She nodded. "Let's clear it up."

"Quack! Quack! Quack!"

Three ducks bobbed past. They were snowy white, but when one of them ruffled her tail, Lily spotted a few gray feathers among the white ones.

"I remember those markings!" Lily whispered excitedly. "We took care of those three ducks in the wildlife hospital when they were little ducklings. Now they're all grown up!"

Lily's parents ran the Helping Paw

Wildlife Hospital in a converted barn in their yard. Jess and Lily loved caring for the injured or orphaned creatures—they both adored animals!

When the ducks had gone, the girls kneeled at the water's edge to gather leaves from some gnarled old tree roots that grew by the stream. Soon they had made a big pile.

"The stream looks much better," said Jess.

She reached out to grab another handful of soggy leaves.

"Jess, listen!" said Lily. "I can hear rustling."

Jess stood up, and gave a delighted cry. "Look!"

A beautiful golden cat bounded out of the cattails, her eyes as green as sunlit grass.

"Goldie!" cried Lily.

The cat pressed against the girls' legs, purring happily.

Goldie lived in a secret world called Friendship Forest. She'd taken the girls on some amazing adventures there, and they'd made lots of animal friends. All the forest creatures lived in adorable little cottages or dens—but best of all, they could talk!

"I wish you could speak in our world, Goldie," said Jess, bending to pet her.

The cat glanced across the stream toward Brightley Meadow, and mewed.

Lily's eyes sparkled. "She wants to take us to Friendship Forest!"

The cat leaped across the stream's stepping stones into Brightley Meadow, and looked back.

"We're coming!" Jess called.

The girls raced after Goldie toward a big, lifeless old tree in the middle of the meadow. The Friendship Tree!

As Goldie drew near, new leaves sprang from every branch. Lily and Jess grinned as a squirrel darted about, gathering fat brown acorns, and a flock of rainbow finches swooped down to chatter noisily

among

the branches.

"It's so

gorgeous!" said Lily.

They hurried to join Goldie, and the cat lifted her paw to pat some letters carved into the trunk.

Jess's tummy fluttered with excitement. "Ready?" she asked.

Lily nodded. Together they read the words. "Friendship Forest!"

A door appeared in the tree trunk. Jess glanced at Lily, then reached out to turn the leaf-shaped handle.

The door opened, and golden light spilled out as the girls followed their friend inside the tree. As the shimmering glow surrounded them, they tingled all over, and knew that they were shrinking, just a little bit.

When the golden light faded, Lily and Jess found themselves in a sun-dappled forest clearing. The air was warm, and the delicious scent of honeysuckle and ripe blackberries drifted on the breeze.

"We're in Friendship Forest!" cried Lily.

The girls turned around to see Goldie. The cat was now standing upright, wearing a golden scarf. She ran to the girls and hugged them. Now that they were smaller, she reached almost to their shoulders.

"I'm so glad you're here," Goldie said.

"Me, too!" Jess said—then she frowned anxiously. "But why have you brought us here, Goldie? Is Grizelda causing trouble?"

Grizelda was a horrible witch who wanted the forest all for herself. Now she had four creatures helping her—a bat, a rat, a toad, and a crow. They came from the Witchy Waste, which had once been a pretty water garden, full of ponds and water lilies. But the creatures were so messy that they'd ruined it! Grizelda had asked them to make Friendship Forest messy, too, so that the animals would have to leave—and then Friendship Forest would be hers.

But luckily, Goldie shook her head.

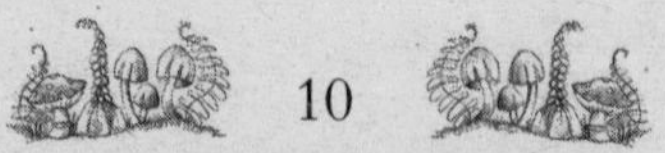

"Nobody's seen Grizelda since your last visit," she told them.

Lily and Jess grinned at each other.

"Phew! That's a relief," said Lily.

"I brought you here for a *much* nicer reason," said Goldie, her green eyes shining. "Agatha Glitterwing the magpie is holding a Craft Club for all the animals at her jewelry shop. Would you like to come and join in with us?"

Lily and Jess glanced at each other in delight. "Yes, please!" they cried.

CHAPTER TWO

An Unwelcome Visitor

The path to Agatha's shop was lined with pink poppies and bright sunflowers. As they walked nearer, a jingly noise floated on the air, like hundreds of tiny bells.

"What's that?" asked Lily. "It sounds so pretty!"

Goldie smiled. "You'll see!"

As they walked around a thicket of bushes, they saw a large beech tree with necklaces and bracelets dangling from every branch. As they stepped closer, Jess and Lily could see that the jewelry was made from shiny seeds, nuts, and pebbles. As the breeze blew, they jingled and jangled like dozens of tiny wind chimes.

"So that's what's making the noise!" cried Lily.

Goldie smiled. "Welcome to Agatha Glitterwing's shop," she said.

Beneath the tree, lots of little animals were sitting on blankets.

"Hey, everyone, it's Jess and Lily!" called out a rabbit wearing a purple ribbon around her neck.

"Lucy Longwhiskers!" Lily cried, recognizing the bunny they'd rescued on their first adventure in Friendship Forest.

There was a chorus of happy, squeaky, squawky greetings.

"I'm so happy you're here!" Sophie Flufftail the squirrel told them as she hugged Jess's leg.

"Me, too!" cried Ruby Fuzzybrush the fox cub.

Agatha Glitterwing fluttered over with

OPEN

an excited squawk. “Welcome to my shop!” she told the girls. When she spoke, her long, shiny necklace jangled. “Would you like to make some jewelry, too? It’s so much fun!”

“We’d love to!” they said, and settled on a blanket next to a sleek little brown otter. She had a long tail and a pretty pointed face with sparkling eyes. Around her neck, she wore a necklace of shiny silver shells.

“I’m Chloe Slipperslide,” she said.

“I love your necklace,” Jess said. “It’s so pretty! Did you make it?”

Chloe beamed. “Thank you! Yes, I

made it at Craft Club! I can help you make necklaces, too, if you like."

"Chloe made this for me," said a small voice. It was a tiny turtle in a violet swimming cap.

"Violet Flippershell!" Lily said, delighted.

Violet held up her flipper. She wore a bracelet of the same silver shells as the otter's necklace. "I love my bracelet. Chloe's so good at making things."

Chloe modestly shook her head, and the tips of her ears blushed pink. She rummaged in a basket, pulled out two ribbons, and passed them to the girls.

"To start your necklace, you need to hold one end of the ribbon," she began.

Snap!

Pebbles, nuts, and seeds suddenly rained down on them from above.

"Oh, no!" cried Chloe, looking up into the branches of Agatha's shop. "One of the necklaces must have broken!"

"What happened?" squawked Agatha.

Snap!

More nuts fell, bouncing off Violet's shell. "Eek!" she squealed in surprise.

"Caw! Caw!"

Everyone looked up to see a scruffy crow perched on a branch above their heads. Jess let out a gasp. "It's Snippit!"

Snippit was one of Grizelda's messy helpers from the Witchy Waste. He wore a waistcoat with a missing button. As the girls watched, he closed his beak around the string of another beautiful necklace. *Snap!* The nuts tumbled to the ground.

"Stop breaking Agatha's jewelry, Snippit!" cried Lily.

"Won't," he cawed. "It's fun!"

Goldie shook the nuts and seeds from her fur. "He's going to make poor Agatha's shop as messy as the Witchy Waste!" she said.

A moment later, the other Witchy Waste creatures came out from the trees. "What a lovely mess you've made, Snippit!" cried Peep the bat, while Masha the rat and

Hopper the toad laughed with glee.

Snippit giggled as he pecked at another necklace. "Heeheehee! I love shiny things, and shiny messes are even better!"

Agatha flapped her wings furiously as more seeds came tumbling down.

"Go on," Masha the rat called to Snippit. "Do it!"

Jess glanced at Lily. "Oh, no," she said, "Masha's telling Snippit to use his spell!"

Grizelda had given each of the Witchy

Waste creatures a magic spell which would make one of the forest animals as messy as they were. If the spell wasn't lifted, the poor animal would completely transform into a Witchy Waste creature just like them! Then it would be able to change another animal, too, until the whole forest was filled with messy creatures.

"Run!" Goldie yelled to the animals. "Quick, before Snippit casts his spell on you!"

The crow was already ruffling his scruffy feathers, and purple sparks were flying around him. The animals fled in panic, rushing to hide in the trees and bushes.

But when Lily looked back, she was horrified to see that Chloe hadn't moved.

"Chloe! Run!" Lily cried.

But Chloe just crouched with her paws over her eyes and her long tail quivering.

"She's too scared to move," cried Jess. "I'll get her!"

But before she could reach Chloe, purple sparks splattered over the frightened little otter.

Lily gasped. "Oh, no! Snippit's put a spell on Chloe!"

CHAPTER THREE

The Wicked Spell

Snippit flew around in circles, cawing with delight as Jess, Lily, and Goldie rushed to Chloe. The purple sparks died away, and the little otter blinked up at them, her eyes wide with worry.

"It's okay," Lily said, picking Chloe up and cuddling her. "We'll stop the spell."

Then Jess spotted an orb of yellow-green light floating toward Agatha's shop. "Oh, no!" she said with a groan. "Look! Grizelda's coming!"

With a flash of smelly sparks, the orb transformed into the witch. She wore a purple tunic over tight black pants and high-heeled boots, and her green hair swirled wildly around her bony face. Snippit landed on her shoulder.

Grizelda stroked Snippit's scruffy head.

"Well done," she told him. "That otter will soon start being messy, too. Then you can spoil the forest together—and the meddling cat and the interfering girls won't be able to stop you! Ha-ha!"

"Yes we will, Grizelda!" Jess shouted. "We stopped Peep's spell, and Masha's, and we'll stop Snippit's, too!"

"Snippit's much smarter than those two." Grizelda sneered. "You won't win this time!" She

threw back her head and laughed, her locks of green hair twisting and swirling about her head. Then she snapped her fingers and vanished in a splatter of stinky sparks. Snippit landed next to the other three Witchy Waste creatures.

Lily turned and called to the animals, "Grizelda's gone!"

They all crept out slowly from their hiding places. Lily glanced at Chloe, who was still in her arms. The tiny otter had a dazed look in her eyes.

"Will she be okay?" Violet Flippershell asked tearfully.

Goldie knelt down next to her. But before she could answer Violet, Snippit swooped over and pecked at a ribbon.

"Leave that alone!" squawked Agatha the magpie. "You've made enough of a mess already!"

"I'm just getting started," Snippit told her, gleefully turning over a basket of ribbons. Then he picked up a little pair of scissors in his beak and stuffed them into his waistcoat pocket!

Agatha's feathers all stood up on end. "That's stealing!" she told him furiously.

Chloe suddenly wriggled out from Lily's arms. She ran to Sophie Flufftail and snatched the seed bracelet the squirrel had been making. Then she flapped her front legs and hopped away into the trees as if she was trying to fly.

"Oh, no!" said Goldie. "The magic's starting to work. Chloe's already behaving just like Snippit!"

"Poor Chloe!" Violet wailed, her head and legs disappearing into her shell.

"We have to do something!" squawked Agatha, her wings flapping madly.

Jess pulled her little sketchbook from her pocket. "Don't worry," she said. "We know exactly what to do! We need the spell we found in Mrs. Taptree's library."

Lily nodded. "It worked for Olivia Nibblesqueak and Evie Scruffypup. Let's hope it works for Chloe!"

Jess flipped to a page in her sketchbook and read aloud. "A spell to turn you back into yourself again:

You want to be yourself again?

Then here's what you must do.

Gather up those favorite things

That mean the most to you.

What do you like to do the most?

What food do you love the best?

And what's your biggest secret?

Now here's a little test.

Put them in your favorite place,

The place you love to be.

If someone names those things aloud,

Yourself once more you'll be."

"Right," said Lily, "we have to find out Chloe's favorite hobby, her favorite food, and her secret."

"Then put them in her favorite place to break the spell!" Jess added. She turned to Goldie. "Let's go and talk to Chloe's family. They'll know what her favorite things are."

"Good idea," said Goldie, "but I'm not sure where they live."

"Should we ask Violet?" suggested Lily. "She's friends with Chloe."

Poor Violet was so upset about Chloe that she was still in her shell. Jess knelt

down and whispered to the little turtle. "We need to find the Slipperslides so we can help Chloe. Can you tell us where they live?"

There was a sniff from inside the shell, then the little violet swimming cap appeared, and the tiny turtle peeped out.

"They live on the Wide Lake," she said, shakily.

"Thanks!" said Jess. "Come on, we've got to lift that spell—before Chloe turns into a naughty crow like Snippit!"

CHAPTER FOUR

The Wide Lake

As the girls and Goldie got to Willowtree River, Lily spotted a lovely silver raft moored to a tree with a long silver ribbon.

"That belongs to Silvia Whitewing the swan and her sisters," she said. "Remember we went on it when we rescued Ellie Featherbill?"

Goldie's ears pricked up. "There they are now!"

Three swans were having a picnic on a lacy cloth beneath a weeping willow.

"Where's the Slipperslides' house?" Lily called to them.

"Why, it's over there," Silvia said, pointing her wing out over the water.

Standing on stilts over the water was a neat wooden house. Fixed to one side were three diving boards and a polished wooden slide.

Two young otters were whizzing down the slide while two more leaped from the diving boards. They all splashed into the water, squealing with delight as they tumbled over one another.

"Thank you!" Lily cried to the swans. The girls and Goldie ran around the lake, waving their arms.

When the otters

spotted them, they swam across. The littlest one, who was wearing pink goggles, was clinging on to her big sister's red swimming cap. When they reached the shore, they turned over and floated on

their backs. The tiny one hooked her paw around her sister's so she wouldn't drift away.

"I'm Flo," said the otter in the red swimming cap. Her two brothers floated

alongside her. "This is Richard and Johnny, and our little sister is Tallulah."

There was a shout from the little house. "Coo-eee!"

"And here come Mom and Dad," added Flo.

A moment later, Mr. and Mrs. Slipperslide appeared at the door. They dove off the highest board and swam swiftly to the bank.

Goldie introduced Jess and Lily.

"It's nice to meet you," said Mr. Slipperslide. "This is all our family except for little Chloe. She's at Craft Club."

"That's why we're here," said Lily. "I'm afraid we have bad news." She explained what had happened.

The young otters crowded around their parents.

"That horrible crow!" wailed tiny Tallulah.

Jess crouched down and took Tallulah's little paw. "Don't worry," she said. "We've got a plan."

Mr. Slipperslide hugged all his children, then looked up at the girls. "How can we help?" he asked. "We'll do anything to save Chloe."

"We need you to answer a few questions," Lily said. "First, what's Chloe's favorite hobby?"

"I know!" said Flo. "Making jewelry!"

"That's right," said Mrs. Slipperslide. "She's very proud of her silver shell necklace. She never takes it off."

Lily turned to Jess. "Chloe's necklace must be her favorite thing," she said, "so we'll need it for the spell. But she's wearing it! How are we going to get it?"

Jess shook her head. "I don't know, but we'll find a way." She turned back to the otters. "We need to find out Chloe's secret, too. Does anyone know what it might be?"

All the Slipperslides shook their heads.

"How about Chloe's favorite place?" asked Lily.

The otters shook their heads again. "This is terrible," said Mrs. Slipperslide. "How are we going to help Chloe?"

"Don't worry," Jess told them. "Do you know what her favorite food is?"

Richard, Johnny, and tiny Tallulah splashed up onto the shore, wriggling about and shouting over the others in excitement. Finally, Flo wriggled past them. "We know that one!" she said. "Rainbow water lily salad! That's Chloe's favorite food!"

"Mine, too!" said Richard.

"And mine!" said Johnny.

"Yum, yum!" squeaked tiny Tallulah.

"That's great," said Jess with a grin. "It sounds delicious. Where do rainbow water lilies grow?"

But to the girls' surprise, the otters all suddenly looked worried.

"There aren't any left around here," said

Mrs. Slipperslide. "We ate the last ones this morning!"

Mr. Slipperslide's whiskers drooped sadly. "There are some on the other side of the Rushing Rapids, but it's too dangerous to swim there. What are we going to do?"

The Slipperslides hugged one another. "Poor Chloe!" cried Flo.

"Don't worry," Goldie told them. "I know how to get past the rapids—on a raft!"

Goldie led the girls back to Silvia and her sisters. They found them looking beneath their lace cloth, in their picnic basket, and even under their wings.

"Where are they?" Silvia muttered.

Then she saw the girls and Goldie. "Have you seen our silver spoons?" she asked. "They've vanished!"

Jess shook her head. "Sorry, no," she said. "We've come to ask for your help. We have to get past the Rushing Rapids. Please, would you take us on your raft?"

But the three swans shook their heads.

"We're very busy," said Silvia.

"We can't eat strawberry mousse without spoons!" said her sister.

"Please, Silvia, it's important," said Lily. She told the swans about Chloe.

"Well, my dear, why didn't you say?" Silvia pointed a wing at the pearl necklace she was wearing. "Little

Chloe mended this for me when it broke. We must help her. Come along!"

They followed the swans to the riverbank. When they reached the water, the girls gasped.

The silver raft was gone!

Silvia ruffled her feathers, clearly upset. "First the spoons go missing, now our raft!" she cried.

Lily and Jess looked up and down the bank. "But it was just here!" Jess cried out.

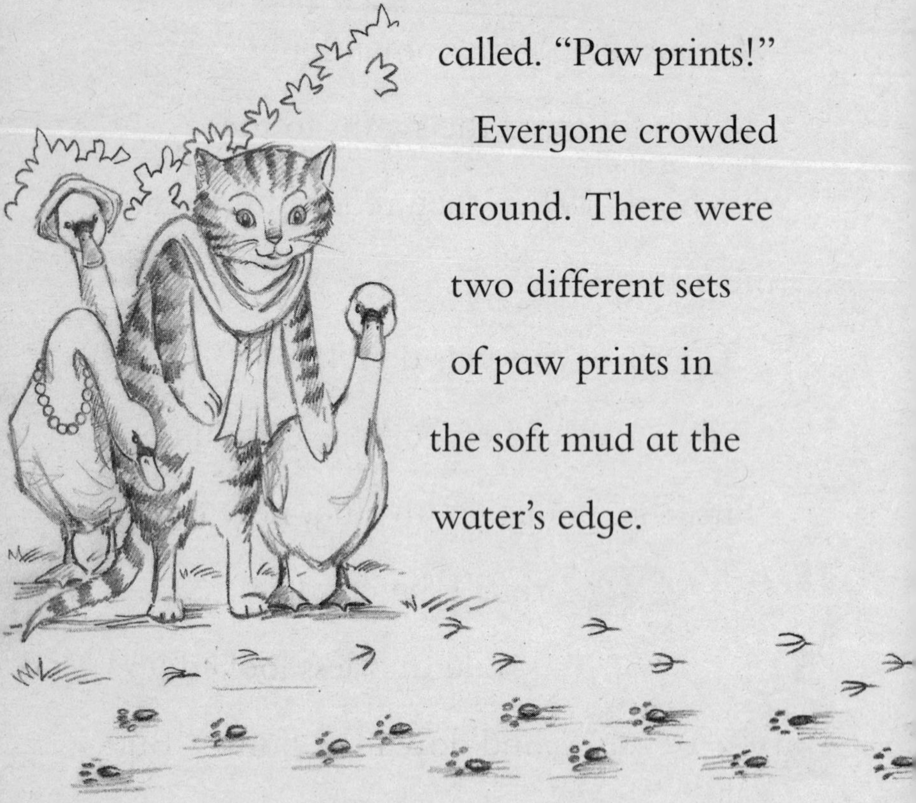

"Look," Goldie called. "Paw prints!"

Everyone crowded around. There were two different sets of paw prints in the soft mud at the water's edge.

Lily peered over Jess's shoulder. "Those must be Snippit's," she said, looking at the

bird prints. "He stole the scissors from Agatha's shop, remember? I bet he's stolen the spoons and the raft, too!"

"And those must be Chloe's," Jess groaned, looking at the other paw prints. "Now how will we get to those water lilies?"

Goldie's ears suddenly pricked up. "What's that noise?" she asked.

The girls listened carefully. "It's quacking!" said Lily.

Around the river bend, a pretty blue-and-yellow barge appeared. A family of ducks stood on deck, waving.

"It's the Featherbills!" cried Jess. "Thank goodness—we can ask them to help us!"

CHAPTER FIVE

Toadstool Glade

"Hello!" Mr. and Mrs. Featherbill and their eight ducklings quacked.

"Can you help us?" Jess called. "We need to get past the Rushing Rapids to save Chloe Slipperslide!"

"Certainly," said Mrs. Featherbill.

"We heard about poor Chloe. What a flapdoodle! Come aboard."

"Good luck!" Silvia the swan called as the girls scrambled on board and the barge moved away from the bank. "We hope you help poor Chloe."

"Thanks! We'll look out for your raft and spoons!" yelled Lily.

"We need to get some rainbow water lilies," Goldie explained to the Featherbill family.

"We'll find them in no time," said Mr. Featherbill. "Don't you worry!"

Mr. and Mrs. Featherbill turned the

tiller, steering the barge out into the center of the lake. Ahead, the water was dark blue and bubbling.

"The Rushing Rapids," called Mrs. Featherbill. "Hold on, everybody!"

The girls and Goldie held onto the railing at the edge of the barge. Little Ellie Featherbill ran to cling to Jess's ankle, and her seven brothers and sisters held onto Lily and Goldie. As they reached the rapids, the barge rocked backward and forward. The ducklings quacked with excitement.

"It's like being on an amusement park ride!" said Lily.

Then the rocking stopped, and the barge was gliding through calm waters once more.

"Look!" cried Lulu Featherbill. "There, in the middle of those green lily pads!"

Jess and Lily craned to look. Rainbow-colored blooms shimmered on the surface of the huge round leaves.

"We found them!" cried Jess.

"We have to stop here," said Mrs. Featherbill. "The barge can't go any closer or we'll damage the lily pads."

Jess and Lily looked at each other in dismay.

"Don't worry! We ducklings are so light we can walk on them," said Ellie.

The ducklings jumped overboard and arranged themselves into a chain, holding one another's wings, as they reached across the lily pads to the flowers in the middle.

"Hooray!" Jess cried as Ellie picked

the first water lily and passed it from duckling to duckling until it reached the girls.

Lily gazed at the gorgeous flower.

The petals really were every color of the rainbow. "It's beautiful," she said.

Once they had enough flowers and the ducklings were safely back on board,

Lily couldn't resist tasting a petal. "It's delicious!" she said. "Like fresh lettuce flavored with ripe blueberries! No wonder these are Chloe's favorite."

"They should be your favorite, too," Ellie said, "because of your name."

Lily smiled and stroked the duckling's feathery head.

The ducks took the friends back through the Rushing Rapids to where they'd picked them up. Goldie and the girls thanked them for their help and waved good-bye.

"We've got Chloe's favorite food," Jess said happily. She looked down at the footprints they'd seen earlier. "Now we just have to find a way to get her necklace! Let's follow these—hopefully they'll lead us to Chloe."

Lily and Goldie agreed, and they set off. Alongside the paw prints were some strange marks, as if something heavy had been dragged along.

"It must have been the swans' raft!" said Lily. "But where were the Witchy Waste creatures taking it?"

"I think it might be to Toadstool Glade!" said Goldie. "Look, we're almost there."

As they entered the glade, they stopped and stared in astonishment. The pretty little cottages and the Toadstool Café were empty. But right in the middle was something huge, silvery, and messy, glittering in the sunlight.

"What is it?" gasped Goldie.

Jess moved closer. It was a huge pile of objects, all thrown on top of one another. "It's an enormous nest," she said, "but it's not built of twigs—it's made of all sorts of shiny things! Pots . . . and pans . . ."

"Silver spoons!" said Lily, pointing. "I bet they're Silvia's."

"And the Whitewings' raft!" Goldie cried. "I'll bet everything here has been stolen!"

"Those naughty creatures," said Jess, shaking her head.

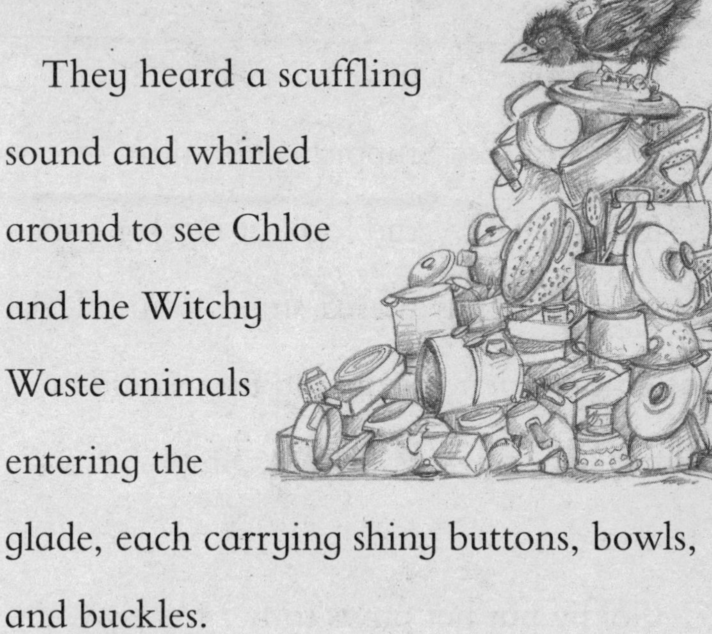

They heard a scuffling sound and whirled around to see Chloe and the Witchy Waste animals entering the glade, each carrying shiny buttons, bowls, and buckles.

Hopper, Masha, and Peep hurried to the nest and stood guarding it while Snippit flew to the top. "Look what Chloe's stolen!" he screeched.

"Heeheehee! I like making a lovely, shiny mess," squawked Chloe.

Lily looked at Jess in dismay. "She sounds just like Snippit!" she said.

Jess nodded. "And look at her fur," she said. Chloe's fur wasn't smooth and sleek anymore—it was sticking up in muddy tufts. "She's just as dirty as Snippit now," Jess said.

Goldie put her paws to her face. "We have to get her favorite necklace and break the spell!"

"I'll do it!" said Jess. She crept up behind Chloe as quietly as she could, then dove for her. But the little otter wriggled free and raced away.

"Missed!" Jess groaned.

"It doesn't matter," said Lily. "Look, she's not wearing her necklace anymore!"

"But now what?" said Goldie. "It could be anywhere!"

"Wait!" said Jess. "The necklace is shiny. I bet Chloe put it on the nest!"

Lily smiled in relief. "That means all we have to do is find it."

Goldie pointed at Hopper, Masha, and Peep, who were still standing close to the nest. "But how are we ever going to get close enough to look?"

CHAPTER SIX

Good Old Mr. Cleverfeather!

As Goldie and the girls were working out what to do, some of the Friendship Forest animals crept back into Toadstool Glade.

Mrs. Longwhiskers held Lily's hand. "They took my frying pan," she said.

"Hard luck!" cawed Snippit.

"I want my jewelry back!" said Agatha Glitterwing.

"They've got my shiny pen!" said Mr. Silverback the badger.

"And we need that necklace," Jess whispered to Lily.

She marched to the nest, but Snippit flew at her, snapping crossly. She quickly stepped back.

When Agatha flew toward the nest, Snippit jabbed at her with his beak.

"If we're going to search for the necklace," Lily said softly, "we have to make those Witchy Waste creatures leave the nest. And Chloe, too."

Jess sighed. "Even if we manage to make them leave, there's too much stuff to search through it all," she said. "We'll never find the necklace quickly enough."

"What's this?" said a familiar voice. "A nettle mest? I mean a metal nest?"

It was their friend Mr. Cleverfeather the owl.

"Hello!" cried Lily. "Maybe you can help us!"

"Goodness! Less and Jilly," he said, getting his words muddled as usual. "I came to look for my telescope. I heard the thinny shings were here. I mean, shiny things."

Jess told him what had happened, and why they needed to find Chloe's necklace.

"Do you have an invention that might help?" Lily asked.

Mr. Cleverfeather put a wingtip to his forehead and frowned in thought. "I've just the thing!" he said. "Sack boon!" he cried, flying off. "I mean, back soon!"

The girls turned back to the nest to see Snippit hopping on top of it. "We need more!" he screeched. "It's not big enough or messy enough yet!"

"That gives me an idea!" Lily whispered to Jess and Goldie. "Let's pretend we know where there are lots of shiny things they could collect."

"Okay," whispered Jess. "Here goes."

They moved closer to the nest, and Jess in a voice just loud enough for Snippit to hear, "It's lucky the animals have hidden their best shiny things behind the flowering plum tree."

"Yes," Goldie replied loudly. "That's right down by the river . . ."

Snippit gave a delighted squawk. "Silly humans!" he said. "Silly cat! Now we know where more shiny things are. Let's get them!"

The Witchy Waste creatures hopped, flew, and scurried away, with Snippit in the lead. Chloe flapped her paws clumsily behind them.

Jess clapped her hands gleefully.

"It worked!" said Goldie. "Snippit isn't as smart as Grizelda thought. Come on, let's find Chloe's necklace!"

The animals joined the girls as they clambered over the nest.

Jess and Lily poked and prodded as they searched, sending shiny things rattling, tumbling, and clanging to the ground.

"My pen!" cried Mr. Silverback.

"And my frying pan!" said Mrs. Longwhiskers.

Goldie and the girls kept searching. After a while, Lily pulled out a telescope.

"Mr. Cleverfeather will be pleased," said Jess. "Here he comes!"

The owl flew down, carrying a little round object with lots of magnifying glasses stuck out of it.

"Lake a took at this," he said. "I mean, take a look. I invented it when Clara Curlyshell the snail got lost. It's my Shell Seeker."

"That's just what we need to find Chloe's necklace!" said Jess. "And here's your telescope, Mr. Cleverfeather."

"You found it!" He beamed. "Dell won! I mean, well done!"

There were two horns sticking out of the top of the machine. Mr. Cleverfeather bent over and spoke into them. "Find silver shells!"

Fooff! With a burst of pink smoke, the Shell Seeker rose up and floated toward the nest. The magnifying glasses twitched this way and that, looking in all directions.

Suddenly, pink smoke puffed—*fooff!*—from the top of the Shell Seeker. The Shell Seeker dived downward, and then the girls heard clatters and rattles as it rummaged around inside the nest. Then there was another loud *fooff!* and it reappeared. An arm was sticking out of it—and it was waving Chloe's necklace!

"Hooray!" cried Lily.

As the Shell Seeker returned, she reached up and got the necklace. Jess grabbed the machine and gave it to Mr. Cleverfeather.

"Janks, Thess," he said. "I mean . . ."

She laughed. "We know what you mean."

"We've got Chloe's favorite food, and her necklace to show her favorite hobby," said Lily. "Now we have to find out her secret and her favorite place. And I think I know how."

Goldie gave a puzzled frown. "Even the other Slipperslides didn't know," she said. "How will we find out?"

"Do you remember how upset Violet Flippershell was when Snippit did his spell?" asked Lily. "That's because she's

Chloe's best friend. We can ask her about the things we need."

Jess grinned. "And as Violet's a turtle," she said, "she'll be easy to find—with the Shell Seeker!"

CHAPTER SEVEN

Violet's Secret

Mr. Cleverfeather balanced his invention on his wingtips. "Seek a green shell!" he told it.

As the Shell Seeker took off through the forest, Goldie and the girls dashed after it.

They ran through the trees. Soon, they could just make out screeches and squeals of rage from the Witchy Waste creatures, coming from the path to the river.

"They must have realized that we tricked them," said Lily. "They sound really mad!"

The Shell Seeker led them back toward the Wide Lake. They left the trees behind and found themselves on a little beach, with soft, powdery sand and shallow pools surrounded by pearly rocks. The lake stretched out before them.

"This place is called Summer Sands," Goldie told them.

The Shell Seeker lay still on the ground.

"It's stopped," said Lily. "That must mean Violet's nearby."

"She is!" cried Jess. "Look, beneath that overhanging rock!"

The little turtle was sitting alone, staring sadly out across the lake.

"Violet!" Lily called.

The turtle turned. "Chloe?" she said excitedly. Then her face fell. "Oh, hello. I'm glad to see you all, but I really miss my friend."

Lily lifted Violet up and hugged her. "We'll find Chloe," she said.

Jess picked up a pair of little yellow armbands, each marked with a *C*. "Are these Chloe's?" she asked.

Violet's head and legs disappeared into her shell. "Well . . ." she mumbled from inside.

Lily stroked her shell. "It's okay. You can tell us," she said.

Slowly, Violet came out again. "She's

the only Slipperslide who isn't very good at swimming," she said, "so I've been giving her lessons here. She's using the armbands until she gets better at it."

Lily grinned in delight. "And these lessons . . . are they a secret?"

When Violet nodded again, Jess popped a kiss on her tiny swimming cap. "Thanks to you, we have almost everything we need to break the spell!"

As they talked about what to do next, Lily noticed some little silver shells on the sand. "Look! They're just like the ones on Chloe's necklace," she said.

Violet sniffed sadly. "This is where she collects shells," she said. "Summer Sands is her favorite place."

Jess and Lily couldn't believe their ears.

"We have everything we need to break Snippit's spell!" said Goldie. "The necklace for Chloe's favorite hobby, the rainbow water lilies for her favorite food, the armbands for her secret, and Summer Sands as her favorite place. Now we can do the spell to change Chloe back to her normal self!"

Jess pulled her sketchbook out and read the end of the spell out loud:

"Put these things in your favorite place,

The place you love to be.

If someone chants the names of those things

Yourself once more you'll be."

She looked up, eyes shining. "We're ready. All we need is Chloe."

"Caw! Caw!"

Lily turned around. "It's Chloe! And Snippit! They must have seen us on their way here and followed us."

The crow was flying low to the ground

alongside Chloe, who was flapping her front paws, hopping and pecking at things with her little brown nose.

"There they are," screeched Snippit angrily. "They tricked us!"

Goldie's tail twitched with worry. "Chloe's really acting like a crow now,"

she cried. "We'd better hurry up and do the spell!"

Jess and Lily placed the necklace, water lilies, and armbands on the sand.

"Look at these, Chloe," Goldie called.

The little otter hopped awkwardly toward the heap. Her eyes widened.

"I think she still remembers them," Jess whispered. "Get ready to say the names of her favorite things!"

But Snippit hopped between Chloe and the pile.

"Come on, Chloe," he cawed. "Let's go and find more shiny stuff to mess up."

He hopped away. Chloe looked from the pile to Snippit, then turned to follow the naughty crow.

"Quick!" Lily cried. "Start chanting the spell now!"

CHAPTER EIGHT

Chloe's Gifts

"Chloe's favorite hobby," Lily chanted. "Making jewelry!"

"Chloe's favorite food," added Goldie. "Rainbow water lilies!"

Jess touched the armbands. "Chloe's secret—swimming lessons!"

"In Chloe's favorite place—Summer Sands!" they all shouted together.

Purple sparks flew from the little otter. As Snippit stared in surprise, the dirt magically disappeared from Chloe's fur, and she was a sleek little otter once more.

She rubbed her eyes."What happened?" she asked. "I feel so strange!"

Jess darted over to scoop her up for a cuddle. "Snippit put a spell on you, but you're safe now," she said.

Chloe gave

a small smile. "Thank you," she said. "I feel better now."

"I don't," Snippit said sadly. "I don't have anyone to help me steal things anymore."

"You shouldn't steal things, Snippit." Goldie said firmly. "It's very, very wrong." She picked up a shiny pebble and held it out to him. "This doesn't belong to anyone. You can have it."

The crow gave a happy squawk. "Thank you!"

"No more stealing, okay?" Jess said.

"Okay," he replied. "I'll find things instead. Like treasure hunting!"

He took off. As he flew away from Summer Sands, a yellow-green orb of light flew toward it.

"Grizelda!" Lily cried in alarm.

The orb floated over the beach and burst into spitting yellow sparks. The witch appeared, stamping her high-heeled boots.

"You've ruined Snippit's spell!" she said, glaring at the girls, "but I've saved my messiest creature till last. Just wait till Hopper casts her spell. You won't believe how disgusting and dirty she'll make Friendship Forest. Then the animals will leave and the forest will be mine!"

"Never!" Lily shouted.

But Grizelda just snapped her fingers and disappeared in an explosion of smelly sparks.

Soon afterward, Jess, Lily, and Goldie were back at Agatha Glitterwing's shop, finishing their necklaces. Violet, Chloe, and the rest of the Slipperslide family were there, too, along with all the other animals. All the scattered seeds and stones had been tidied up, and Agatha was already stringing some new necklaces up in the branches.

"Thank you so much for saving our daughter," said Mr. Slipperslide.

Mrs. Slipperslide hugged Chloe. "We're so happy she's safe," she said, "and we're thrilled she's having swimming lessons!"

Chloe smiled happily as she helped Lily with her necklace. "Mom and Dad said it doesn't matter if I'm not good at swimming," she said. "But if I practice a lot, maybe I can get better!"

"I'm sure you will," said Jess. "But even if you're not the best swimmer, you're already great at making jewelry."

Agatha nodded and twirled her own

necklace thoughtfully. "Chloe," she said, "the jewelry you make is so pretty. Would you like to sell it in my shop?"

The little otter wriggled with excitement. "Yes, please!" she squealed.

Lily and Jess grinned, and all the Slipperslides looked like they would burst with pride.

Chloe hugged Jess, Lily, and Goldie. "I want to give you something to say thank you," she said. Taking three silver shells from her necklace, she looped them each on a chain and gave them to Goldie, Lily, and Jess.

"Chloe, they're gorgeous," said Lily as she put hers on and hugged the otter, who gave a great yawn.

"Bedtime," said Mrs. Slipperslide, "before you fall asleep right here. You've had a very long day."

Jess giggled. "We have to go, too."

They kissed Chloe, and hugged all their other friends.

"Bye!" they called, waving as Goldie took them back to the Friendship Tree.

She touched a paw to the trunk, and opened the door that appeared. Golden light spilled out from inside.

The girls hugged Goldie. "There will be trouble when Hopper casts her spell," said Lily, "but we'll be ready to help."

"I know you will," said Goldie. "Thank you for being such good friends. Good-bye for now! See you soon!"

They stepped into the golden glow and felt the tingle that meant they were returning to their normal size.

Moments later, they were back in Brightley Meadow, heading toward the stream.

"Chloe would love it here," said Lily.

Jess giggled. "We might have to add a slide to one of the trees, though, like the one at the Slipperslides' house!"

"Or a diving board!" Lily laughed. "What an amazing adventure that was!"

Jess grinned back. "I can't wait for our next one!" she said, and together they ran back to Helping Paw.

The End

Little lamb Grace Woollyhop is busy getting ready for a concert at Harmony Hall—until wicked witch Grizelda casts a spell on her!

Now instead of making music, Grace just wants to make trouble! Can Jess and Lily break the spell in time for the concert? Find out in their next adventure,

Grace Woollyhop's Musical Mystery

Turn the page for a sneak peek . . .

"Hide, Grace!" called Goldie.

But it was too late. Hopper had spotted her! The toad sprang toward Grace and she froze, looking terrified.

"Grace, run!" shouted Jess.

But the lamb's legs were shaking too much. "Maa!" she bleated.

Before anyone could move, Hopper's long, flat tongue flicked out. Immediately, purple sparks showered over poor, trembling Grace.

"Oh, no!" cried Lily. "Hopper's cast her spell. Now Grace will start making messes just like a toad!"

The sparks faded. For a moment, the lamb's sweet woolly face looked surprised. Then she grinned and bounded around the shop, knocking over the rest of the balls of wool that were stacked around the shop. They tumbled down and unraveled, making a mess all over the floor.

Read

Grace Woollyhop's Musical Mystery

to find out what happens next!

Visit Friendship Forest, where animals can talk and magic exists!

Special Edition!

Meet best friends Jess and Lily and their adorable animal pals in this enchanting series from the creator of Rainbow Magic!

SCHOLASTIC

scholastic.com

MAGICAF2

Puzzle Fun!

Chloe Slipperslide has made Goldie a gorgeous shell necklace! Can you help her find it?

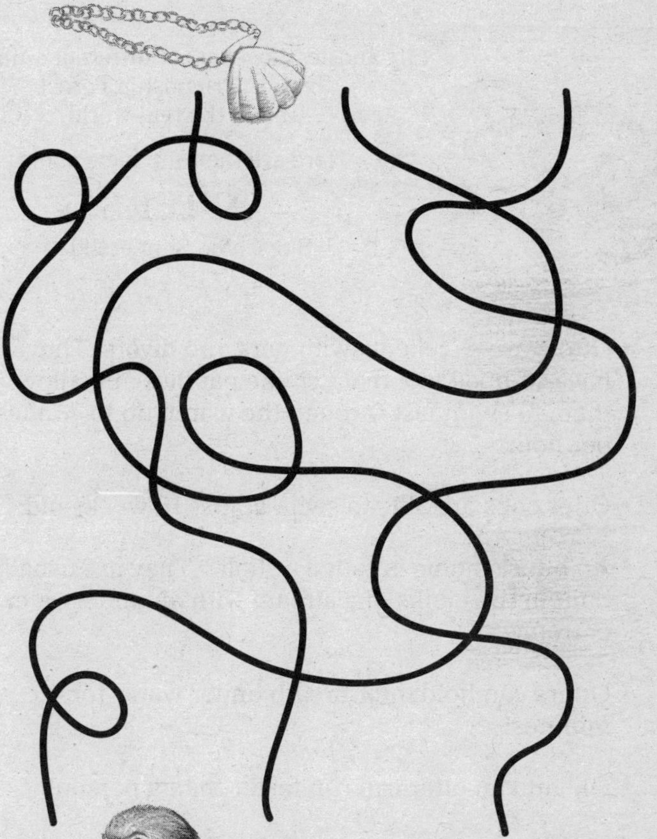

A) B) C)

ANSWER

Path B) leads to Chloe's necklace

Lily and Jess's Animal Facts

Lily and Jess love lots of different animals—
both in Friendship Forest
and in the real world.

Here are their top facts about

OTTERS

like Chloe Slipperslide.

- Otters are excellent swimmers and divers. They have webbed feet that act like paddles and allow them to swim fast through the water, up to 7 miles per hour!
- Otter cubs are able to swim at just 10 weeks old.
- An otter's home is called a "holt." They are usually built in the banks of a stream with an underwater entrance.
- Otters can hold their breath under water for 8 minutes!
- On land an otter can run faster than a person!